To:

Autumn

Always love others.

Gary Chapman

5-26-12

A Perfect Pet
for Peyton

#1 *New York Times* Bestselling Author
GARY CHAPMAN

& RICK OSBORNE ♥ Illustrated by WILSON WILLIAMS, JR.

NORTHFIELD
PUBLISHING

ISBN: 978-0-8024-0358-2
Printed by R R Donnelley in Willard, Ohio — March, 2012

The Lightwave Team:
Project manager: Luba Osborne
Creative director: Rick Osborne
Cover design: Kathryn Joachim
Interior design: Jill Ronsley
Cover illustrations: Wilson Williams Jr.
Editing: Ed Strauss
Proof readers: Luba Osborne, Danica Everts and Romana Osborne
Our perfect pet pals: Buddy, Hunter and Bob

We hope you enjoy this book from Northfield Publishing.
Our goal is to provide high-quality, thought-provoking books and products
that connect truth to your real needs and challenges.
For more information on other books and products written and produced
from a biblical perspective, go to www.moodypublishers.com or write to:

Northfield Publishing
820 N. LaSalle Boulevard
Chicago, IL 60610

Library of Congress Cataloging-in-Publication Data

Chapman, Gary D.,
    A perfect pet for Peyton : a 5 love languages discovery book / Gary D. Chapman, Rick Osborne.
        p. cm.
    Summary: Twins Peyton and Penny spend their birthday with friends at Mr. Chapman's Perfect Pet Pal Emporium,
where each is to be matched with a special pet based on their own personal love language, but Peyton fears there is no
perfect pet for him. Includes a "Five Love Languages Quiz for Kids."
    ISBN 978-0-8024-0358-2 (hardback)
    [1. Love--Fiction. 2. Pets--Fiction. 3. Birthdays--Fiction. 4. Parties--Fiction. 5. Brothers and sisters--Fiction. 6. Twins--
Fiction.] I. Osborne, Rick. II. Title.
PZ7.C36677Per 2012
[E]--dc23
                                                        2011047250

                                        1 3 5 7 9 10 8 6 4 2
                            Printed in the United States of America

"Get out of bed, sleepyhead! **Today is OUR day!"**

It was a very, very special day indeed! The twins, Peyton and Penny, knew what they wanted to do and had dropped a lot of hints.

"I hope our hints worked," Penny said excitedly.

Peyton stretched. "Me too, but Mom and Dad have been acting like they haven't heard us at all. **Surprises** are so hard to wait for." Peyton sniffed the air. "Wow! Mom's pancakes!"

The twins dashed downstairs.

Happy Birth~~day~~

"Happy Birthday, Peyton and Penny!"

BIRTHDAY KING!!

Find the Insects:
There's at least one insect in every big picture in this book. See if you can find them all. Have fun!

Penny prayed a breakfast prayer and dropped another hint by thanking God for their *birthday adventure*.

Dad chuckled. "Guess where we're going today."

Peyton felt like he'd burst. "Mr. Chapman's **Perfect Pet Pal Emporium?**"

Penny added, "Please, please, please?"

Mom smiled and simply said, "Yes."

The kids exploded with excitement. They were going to the most amazing pet store on the **planet!** It was like a zoo, a museum, a theme park, and a birthday party palace all in one place.

Shortly afterward, Peyton held the door of the **family truck** open for his mom and sister. Penny climbed in right next to her dad. "Dad, did you hear ALL our hints?"

"Oh, we heard ALL your hints," Dad teased. "You're having a party there …" (the twins cheered again) "…*and* getting perfect pet pals."

This time Peyton's cheer wasn't so loud. Mr. Chapman matched each customer with the perfect pet. Peyton knew that Penny really wanted a perfect pet pal to **spend time** with, but he didn't think pet matching would work for *him*. He was just really excited about their party.

Mom grinned. "There's also a surprise you didn't hint about. Your friends' parents are getting them pets as well."

"**Cool!**" Penny said.

How many of these animals can you find outside the Pet Pal Emporium?
Brontosaurus, Grizzly Bear, Emperor Penguin, Giraffe, Bald Eagle, Caribou, Kangaroo, Rabbit

THE PERFECT PET PAL *Emporium*

Animals follow Mr. Chapman wherever he goes.
Can you name the ones following him now?
(There are seven animals to find.)

Peyton opened the colossal doors. He had always wanted a super pet—like a circus animal or a horse—that could do tricks and helpful things. He didn't want just a regular pet, even if everyone else was getting one.

"You must be Peyton and Penny," Mr. Chapman said. "I hear you're getting perfect pet pals today."

"I'm not so sure," Peyton answered.

Just then a super-cute monkey surprised the twins with **bags of jelly beans**. Penny squealed.

"Your birthday guests are inside exploring," said Mr. Chapman.

Penny and Peyton were already moving.

Attractions

(10)

WELCOME!

The twins scanned the map. Penny really wanted to visit the Petting Zoo and the Sea area with its aquarium **tunnels**. Peyton was curious about all the birds. He also didn't want to miss the Reptile area; it had life-size models of dinosaurs that moved.

"Where do you want to start, sis? It's ginormous!"

"Let's hang out together and take turns choosing," Penny answered.

As they set off to explore, they heard an incredible **symphony** of animal sounds that seemed to be calling them on.

The bird area was first. It was a pretty paradise filled with beautiful bird songs, bright colors, and **flapping wings**.

Penny smiled from ear to ear as her good friend Jayla came **skipping** toward her. She loved spending time with Jayla.

"Happy birthday!" Jayla said. "You chose the perfect party place! You two are awesome!"

"Awwwk! Awesome!" said an African Grey Parrot.

"I love that bird," Jayla gushed and they all laughed.

Can you find these birds?
Cockatoo, Duck, Ducklings, Amazon Green Parrot, African Grey Parrot, Sun Parakeet, Yellow Canary, Red Canary, Heron, Puffin, Flamingo, Toucan, Hummingbird

Jayla sniffed and sneezed as they entered the Barnyard area. "Wow! They even make the areas *smell* right," she exclaimed.

"Where's the Petting Zoo?" Penny wondered.

"Arrff!" A helpful dog brushed past Peyton and pushed a gate open. The sign said: **Petting Zoo.**

"Good boy!" Jayla praised.

Penny spotted Sofia, another one of her friends. She was cuddling a large brown and white rabbit.

"**Huggy Birthday,**" sang Sofia. She gave out one-arm hugs, then showed her friends which animals were the softest, furriest, and best to pet.

How many of these animals can you find?
Pig, Rooster, Chicken, Rabbit, Border Collie,
Llama, Chicks, Goat, Sheep, Cow, Horse, Mouse

As they headed to the Aquarium, Peyton noticed that Penny and Sofia were being followed. They giggled gleefully when he handed them their furry animal followers to pet.

At the center of the spectacular sea area, dolphins did tricks and helpful things for the **Aquarium** staff. *A dolphin would be the perfect pet for me*, Peyton thought. He felt a little disappointed that he couldn't take home the kind of animals he really liked.

Can you find these underwater creatures?
Starfish, Great White Shark, Blue Whale, Dolphin, Seahorse, Clown Fish, Stingray, Surgeon Fish, Jellyfish, Schooling Bannerfish

Peyton headed to the Reptile area. Dinosaurs would cheer him up. He was happy to see his friend Kevin there.

"Bappy Hirthday!" Kevin shouted. "Wait until you see your present! And, did you see that cool monkey? He gave me jelly beans."

The girls arrived just as the boys finished their **secret handshake**.

Mr. Chapman followed them in. "I see you found each other. The party starts in ten minutes."

"Thanks," said Jayla. "That's nice of you to tell us." Then she screamed as a robot **dinosaur** nuzzled her shoulder.

Can you find these reptiles and dinosaurs?
Gecko, Tortoise, Apatosaurus, Stegosaurus, Pteranodon, Tyrannosaurus Rex, Green Tree Python, Green Tree Frog, Nile Monitor Lizard

Can you find all of the pretend creepy crawlers on the pizza?
Wasp, Grasshopper, Dragonfly, Red Ant, Caterpillar, Horned Beetle, Black Ant, Ladybug, Stick Bug, Tarantula

The kids were still laughing when they sat down.

"It wasn't *that* funny," Jayla said. Penny sat next to her mom until the pizza arrived.

"We call this our **Cheesy Double Cheeseburger Pizza,**" Mr. Chapman announced. "This one is our **Crazy Creepy Crawlers Creation.**" He laughed. "Just pick the spiders off if you don't want them."

Sofia squirmed even though the bugs weren't real. Peyton stood up and started handing out pieces.

Jayla loved it. "You two have the **best parties!**"

What came next made everyone **gasp**.

Can you figure out where each of these mythical creatures is around the sundae?
Unicorn, Dragon, Gryphon, Centaur, Troll
Seven-headed Dragon, Bigfoot, Mermaid, Leviathan

"It's our **Mythical Monster** Sundae," Mr. Chapman explained. "Chocolate Chunk and Cherry ice cream, covered with Candy-Bar Crumble and **Raspberry Liquid Lava Sauce**. Topped with Red Rippled Whipped Cream, Cotton Candy Smoke and Exploding Rocks. Surrounded, of course, by Mythical Creatures made from sugar."

Sofia gave the twins cheek-to-cheek happy-hugs while everyone sang **Happy Birthday**.

"This is even better than the pizza!" Jayla exclaimed as Peyton helped **scoop out** the sundae.

"**Time** for presents!" Kevin said as he stacked the wrapped packages on the table.

The friends always gave each other **silly gifts.**

This time, Jayla gave the twins plush hippopotamuses that spoke when poked. They said, "You're the **hippoMOSTamus!**"

Kevin gave them huge, **silly hats** that made everyone laugh.

Sofia gave them each a homemade **"Book of Hugs"** for keeping track. "My record is 55 hugs in one day," Sofia announced.

Penny spent time with each of her friends talking about the **great gifts.**

POP! POP! POP!

The kids swung around to see a performer with balloons, a pin and a sneaky smile.

"Balloon fun for everyone!" he said in a high, squeaky voice.

He started twisting **balloons** together in a blur of speed.

"Sweet!" Jayla exclaimed when he handed her a **giraffe**. Sofia loved her **lion** and stroked its balloon mane. Kevin thought his **gorilla** was a great gift.

Peyton helped hold balloons and was rewarded with an enormous **elephant**.

Penny introduced her jaguar to the friendly cat.

Peyton looked at his balloon animal. *A real elephant would be a perfect pet for me. They're smart, do tricks and help people. But where would it sleep?*

"It's time for your ride on the **Jungle Safari** Mountain Roller Coaster," Mr. Chapman announced.

Everyone hollered "Yay!" and headed towards the ride.

The roller coaster **clattered** and climbed up inside the mountain, passing jungle animals of all sorts. Then it plummeted back down and splashed through the river, spraying everyone. Peyton got soaked.

Find the animals:
Elephant, Rhinoceros, Flamingo,
Hippopotamus, Lion

Peyton wasn't very happy. He was wet and wondering what he'd do while everyone else was getting a perfect pet pal. The helpful dog had given him a towel; Peyton covered his head with it.

Mr. Chapman stepped up onto a stump in front of a **curtain of leafy vines**. Everyone, including the parents and even the animals, hushed.

"I believe pets should be perfect pet pals. So, what's a perfect pet pal? Let me explain." Mr. Chapman held up **five fingers**. "There are five ways that people give and receive love. I call them the Five Love Languages."

"**Each** of us especially likes to love and be loved in one or two of these languages; some love kind words, others like touch. Some enjoy spending special time with people. Others love gifts and some like to do nice and helpful things. We all need to **love people** in every way. However, God made us each special and we all love a little differently. Pets do some things **naturally** that can kind of match our Love Language. When you find one that matches yours, that's a perfect pet pal."

The little animals are following Mr. Chapman around as usual. Can you find these?
Lizard, Rabbit, Parakeet, Mouse, Ferret, Hamster

The Five Love Languages are:
Quality Time, Words of Affirmation, Gifts,
Physical Touch and Acts of Service.

"You'll understand better if we just start doing some perfect pet pal matching."

The kids loudly agreed. Peyton shivered.

Mr. Chapman continued, "I've talked to your parents and we're ready to start. Kevin, do you like gifts?"

"I really do!"

"You were quite **thrilled** when the monkey gave you jelly beans. Also, you seemed more excited about the birthday presents than the twins were."

Everyone laughed—it was true!

"Finally, you obviously treasure your **balloon** gift. Who knows which Love Language Kevin speaks?"

Everyone called out, "Gifts!"

Mr. Chapman whistled and the jelly bean monkey ran out through the leafy curtain. He climbed onto Kevin's shoulder and handed him a **banana**.

Kevin could hardly breathe. "Really?" he whispered, not believing it.

Mr. Chapman grinned. "Monkeys don't usually make good pets but this one is a specially trained **Capuchin monkey**. His name is Chipo, which means 'gift.' He loves gifts too and he's your perfect pet pal."

Everyone cheered.

Peyton was amazed. *A monkey would be a perfect pet pal for me too*, he thought.

"**Jayla,** would you like to go next?" Mr. Chapman asked.

"Yes," she answered. "How nice of you!"

Mr. Chapman smiled. "Jayla's Love Language is easy. Since she got here, she's hardly stopped **complimenting** the twins and their party. She's used kind words to encourage pretty much everyone here, including me. Her words make people feel wonderful. Even the hippopotamuses she gave the twins said, 'You're the HippoMOSTamus!' Can you tell me which **Love Language** Jayla likes to speak?"

Everyone guessed and Mr. Chapman agreed.

"Jayla's Love Language is 'Words of Affirmation,' or kind words." Then Mr. Chapman squawked. The African Grey **Parrot** that Jayla saw earlier flew out and onto her shoulder. "Rrawk. Pretty girl!" Jayla was speechless.

Mr. Chapman explained, "Her name is 'Pamela' which means 'all **sweetness**.' She speaks sweet words and she's your perfect pet pal."

"She's amazing!" Jayla gasped. "She's amazing!" Pamela repeated.

Everyone burst out **laughing**.

These are great pets! Peyton thought.
Maybe I can get a perfect pet pal after all.

Sofia was next. She was so happy she ran and hugged her mom.

Mr. Chapman smiled. "Sofia gives hello-hugs, bear hugs, one-arm-while-holding-a-rabbit hugs, cheek-to-cheek hugs and even **happy-hugs**. She even hugs herself."

Sofia giggled.

"Today Sofia held her friends' hands and used her touch to try and cheer one of them up. She's also apparently an expert Petting Zoo person. Kids, are you ready to guess Sofia's Love Language?"

"Physical Touch!"

"Right again."

Peyton was getting excited. Then he **remembered:** *Oh no, I think I told Mr. Chapman that I didn't want a perfect pet pal.*

Mr. Chapman continued, "Sometimes people and their perfect pet pals manage to find each other." Then he made a *tsk* sound.

The large brown and white rabbit appeared. In two huge hops she was in Sofia's huggy arms.

"She's a **French Lop Rabbit.** Her name is Snuggles because, just like you, she loves touch."

"Oh, I was SOOO hoping it would be you!" Sofia said, **giggling.**

"Finally, it's Penny's turn," Mr. Chapman announced.

Penny clapped her hands.

Peyton was suddenly quite sad. *I'm really not getting a perfect pet pal,* he thought.

Mr. Chapman went on. "Penny arrived sitting close to her dad in their **truck**. She wanted to spend time exploring the Emporium with her brother. Then she spent special time with each of her friends to thank them for their gifts. She even had her balloon jaguar spend some **quality** time with the cat."

Everyone laughed.

"TIME to guess."

"QUALITY TIME!"

"Right! Penny loves to spend special time with the ones she loves." Then Mr. Chapman made a *sppss, sppss* sound.

Penny stood up and screamed with excitement. She knew. Her friend the cat **sprinted out,** sprang into her arms and went limp. Penny twirled him around, squealing with joy.

"This is Horace," Mr. Chapman said. "He's a **Rag Doll cat.** His name means 'time.' He will follow you everywhere because he wants to spend time with you."

Find the Animals:
Parrot, Mouse, Ferret,
Guinea Pig, Grass Snake, Rabbit

"Mr. Chapman," Peyton asked timidly. "Am I going to get a perfect pet pal?"

CRASH! Bang. Bang. **CRASH!!!** Everyone looked around. A chef's hat poked out of the kitchen. "I'm sorry, Sir, but you're needed."

"Nothing to worry about, everyone," Mr. Chapman said. **"Mortimer,** our moose, probably just got into the pantry again."

The helpful dog pushed the **kitchen door** open.

"Oh, this is Alex. I'm sure he'll help out while I'm gone," Mr. Chapman said and rushed out.

Peyton sighed and thought, *now I'll never get a perfect pet pal.*

Everyone was quiet. Peyton quickly wiped a tear from his eye and started to gather the discarded wrapping paper. He crumpled up the first **bunch**. Alex trotted over and took it from his hands.

Peyton collected more as Alex put the **first** bunch in the trash can. The dog pushed the boxes together in a pile and took the second bunch of papers to the trash.

Then Alex found Peyton's towel and brought it to him to warm him up. Penny broke the **silence.**

Penny laughed. Her brother stared at her then sat down and quietly started to cry. Penny wrapped her arms around Peyton and Alex.

"Alex is your **perfect pet pal,** Peyton!" Penny said.

All of a sudden everyone saw it. Alex was the perfect pet for Peyton.

"That's right!" exclaimed Jayla. "He's helpful just like you. You're always doing wonderful things for others, like picking up furry followers, holding doors, and serving food."

"Rrawk! **Wonderful things!**" repeated Pamela.

Chipo put a bow on Alex's collar.

"He's your gift buddy," Kevin agreed.

Sofia patted Peyton's back and Snuggles nuzzled his ear.

"**Right** again!" Mr. Chapman said, returning. "Peyton, your Love Language is **Acts of Service**. You're always doing nice things for others. Alex means 'helper.' He's no ordinary pet. He's a well-trained and very clever **Border Collie**. He does tricks, recognizes dozens of commands and he's *always* doing helpful, kind things. I think everyone would agree, he's the perfect pet for Peyton."

Peyton gave Alex a huge hug. He *was* perfect! The place **exploded** with cheers.

That night Dad served leftover pizza.

"Thank you, God, for pizza and for perfect pet pals," Peyton prayed. "And thanks for making us special with Love Languages. Amen."

"No hints?" Dad asked, grinning.

"Well, **Christmas** is coming," Penny teased.

Alex put the twins' Christmas stockings on Mom's knee.

She smiled. "How did he know what to bring?"

The twins **exchanged winks.** Alex barked and took Horace for a circus ride around the kitchen. Everyone laughed. The twins' birthday had been a very special day indeed.

The Five Love Languages Quiz for Kids

We hope you enjoyed this story. Helping kids understand the Five Love Languages will enable them to give and receive love more easily, and this will strengthen your family in turn.

The quiz that follows is a tool to aid you in this endeavor. Before guiding your children through it, we suggest that you read the story several times with them. Talk with them about it and discover which characters and perfect pet pals they are drawn to. Observe which characters they mimic. Reading, watching and talking will give you an idea of which Love Languages your child speaks most.

Once you're comfortable that you've narrowed it down to two, take your children through those quiz questions and discuss their answers with them. When you read the story again, take them through one or two of the other sets of questions. Keep track of their answers. The lists they respond to the most positively should correspond to their primary Love Languages.

Be careful not to put too much emphasis on which language is theirs. Guide them to learn and discover for themselves. Once they've decided, have fun showing them your love in their language. Enjoy the wonderful moments that are created when they realize what you're doing!

Gifts

1. Do you like it a lot when someone gives you a gift?
2. Do you love giving gifts to others?
3. Do you take good care of the gifts you get?
4. Do you remember the last gift that someone gave you?
5. Do you like it when people give you even little gifts like a drawing, a flower, or something they made?
6. Do you give gifts like those to others?
7. Are the gifts you get more special to you than other things you own?

Words of Affirmation

1. Do you like it when people say nice things about you?
2. If you want to make someone feel special do you say nice things to them?
3. Do you often say "thank you" to people?
4. Do you feel good when someone says something nice about you?
5. Do you like it when people say nice things about something you made or did?
6. Do you hope people will say nice things about you and the things you do?
7. Do you say nice things about your friends to other people?

Quality Time

1. Do you like to take your parents to your room to play or to show them something?
2. If you want to make someone feel good do you do spend time with him or her?
3. Do you like being alone with a friend—just the two of you?
4. Do you feel good when someone spends time with you?
5. Do you like it when someone takes you somewhere special?
6. Do you like to go for a drive alone with one of your parents?
7. Do you like talking with one person better than a group of people?

Physical Touch

1. Do you like hugs a lot?
2. Do you like gentle massages?
3. Do you like to hold hands with your friends and family members?
4. Girls: Do you like kisses? Boys: Do you like wrestling?
5. Do you like having your back scratched?
6. When you're with your parents, do you like to sit near them or would you rather your arms and shoulders touched theirs?
7. If you want to make someone feel special do you hug that person?

Acts of Service

1. Do you like helping others?
2. Do you like it when people help you do things?
3. Do you like to ask people to do things for you?
4. Do you like it when people ask you to help them?
5. Do you remember more than one time when someone did something special for you or helped you?
6. If you want to make someone feel special do you *do* something for that person?
7. Do you feel good when someone does something special for you?

Find the Love Language Quiz for adults at 5LoveLanguages.com

Gary Chapman, PhD, is author of the *New York Times* #1 bestselling *The 5 Love Languages*® and the director of Marriage and Family Life Consultants, Inc. Gary travels the world presenting seminars, and his radio programs air on more than 300 stations. Connect with Gary online at: 5lovelanguages.com, /5lovelanguages, /drgarychapman

Rick Osborne is a bestselling author and/or coauthor of more than fifty popular parenting and children's books and products, including *Teaching Your Child How To Pray, Focus on the Family's Parent's Guide to the Spiritual Growth of Children, The Singing Bible* (SingingBible.com), and *The Boys Bible*. Find Rick, his blog, and more great stuff for your family at ChristianParentingDaily.com. Follow Rick at: /rickosborne

Wilson Williams, Jr. has been illustrating for children since he was a child himself and he adores it! Doing it as a career, is a dream come true. A graduate of Ringling School of Art and Design, he currently lives on Merritt Island, Florida. You can see more of his work and contact him at DoubleWIllustrations.com.

If you've enjoyed this book please tell others.